CinderHazel
The Cinderella of Halloween

Deborah Nourse Lattimore

SCHOLASTIC INC.
New York Toronto London Auckland Sydney
Mexico City New Delhi Hong Kong Buenos Aires

This book was originally published in hardcover by the Blue Sky Press in 1997.

ISBN 0-439-39471-6

12 11 10 9 8 7 6 5   5 6 7/0

Printed in the U.S.A.   40

First Scholastic trade paperback printing, September 2002

The text type in this book was set in Heatwave.
Designed by Marijka Kostiw

To

DOLORES JOHNSON, NINA KIDD, and KATHY HEWITT,

artists who aren't afraid of dirt or paint

It was another day in the dustbin for Hazel.

While her two snobby stepsisters, Hermione and Hildy,
had fun casting spells and muttering curses,
it was Hazel's job to clean the floor.
Hazel swept from one end of the room to the other
until the entire floor was covered with a thick layer of dust and dirt.

"You know, Hazel," said Hermione, "instead of sweeping,
you could fly that broom."
"I'm no good at flying it," said Hazel.
She scooped up a panful of ash and poured it right on top of her head.
"This is what I'm good at!" bellowed Hazel. "D-I-R-T!"

"You are disgusting! Absolutely yucky!" said her stepmother.
"All you think about is dirt. For all the time you spend in that
fireplace, we ought to call you Cinderhazel."
"Ooooh, *would* you?" asked Hazel.

That very night, while Cinderhazel played jacks with dirty lumps of coal,
her stepmother and stepsisters got all spiffed up.
They combed their frightful hair and
coated their shoes with very clean shoe tar.
"Going somewhere?" asked Cinderhazel.
"Why, tonight's the Witches' Halloween Ball," said Hermione.
"And," said Cinderhazel's stepmother, "rumor has it
that Prince Alarming might come out of hiding tonight."

"Yes," chortled Hildy. "And he's looking for a bride.
But Cinderhazel, you can't come. We don't want to be seen with you."
"That's right," added Hermione. "You're so messy you'd make us look bad."
"Girls, girls," said the stepmother. "Cinderhazel couldn't get there
if she wanted to. Just look at that cracked broom!" The three of them laughed
and laughed. Then they leaped onto their brooms and blasted out the window.
"Oh, who cares?" muttered Cinderhazel. "Who wants to dance
with some hoity-toity prince anyway?"

But as the night grew darker and darker, Cinderhazel started to simmer.
"Think they can tell me what to do? I'll show them!"
Cinderhazel squished her hat on her head,
grabbed her broom, and jumped on.
Ker-rrrrrack! Snap! The broom broke.

Cinderhazel growled. She crossed her eyes. She crossed her fingers.
She crossed her legs and twisted around in a circle.
POOF! Cinderhazel's hat turned into a pile of dirt.
"Ah, nuts!" yelled Cinderhazel. "I'm staying home.
Besides, there's not a single thing I'd like over at the palace."
"That's what you think," said a voice.
"Who's there?" asked Cinderhazel.

A big cloud of smoke exploded in the middle of the room.
There stood a short, plump witch dressed in dirty dishrags.
"Wow! Great clothes!" said Cinderhazel. "Who are you?"
"I'm your witchy godmother," replied the witch.
"And I can't believe you're not going to the Ball.
Didn't you know there are fifteen filthy fireplaces over there?"

"Really?" asked Cinderhazel.

"Really," said the witch. "And there's something else your stepsisters didn't mention: Prince Alarming is the King of Dirt. If I were you, I wouldn't let them keep you from going."

"By my witchy wig, you're right!" pronounced Cinderhazel.

Then she frowned at her broken broom.

"Step aside," said the godwitch. "This is *my* job."
She waved her arms around her head and said:

"Bad old bats and a toad that's meaner,
Make this broom a vacuum cleaner!"

BOOM! The broom vanished, and in its place sat
a nice, slightly used Hoopler vacuum cleaner.

"Now toot off to meet your Prince," said the godwitch.

"And remember: my spells don't work past midnight."

Cinderhazel sat down on the canister, grabbed the hose, and pulled back.

Va-roooom, vroom, vroom went the vacuum cleaner.

It flew up the chimney, with Cinderhazel on it.

Cinderhazel zoomed across the sky toward the palace.
A magnificent trail of charcoal smoke billowed behind her.

With a downward twist on the hose, Cinderhazel
and her vacuum swooped down the biggest chimney she'd ever seen.

Cinderhazel landed on the hearth of the grand ballroom.
The party was in full swing, and Cinderhazel was full of dirt.
Cinderhazel was so yucky that even she wouldn't have known herself.
"Look!" cried her stepsister Hermione, pointing at the mess
that was Cinderhazel. "It's that dirty Prince!"

"Oooh!" squealed Hildy. "The Prince came out of hiding at last!"
"Princey! Princey!" all the witches cried
as they tugged Cinderhazel out of the fireplace.

"Hey, wait a minute!" cried Hermione, squinting at the dirty face.
"That's not the Prince! That's my stepsister, Cinderhazel!"
"What's that thing with her?" asked Hildy. "It looks like a vacuum cleaner!
Ha, ha, ha!" She guffawed until everyone was laughing.
But across the ballroom, two beady little eyes were watching
from behind a trash can.

"Stop that laughing, or I'll put a spell on you," growled Cinderhazel.
This made everyone roar even louder.
So Cinderhazel crossed her eyes. She crossed her fingers.
She crossed her legs and twisted around in a circle.
POOF! All the witches' broomsticks turned to dirt.

Dust covered everyone in the room.
The witches were furious. "Clean up this mess,
or we'll put a spell on *YOU!*" they screamed.
"Oh, phooey!" said Cinderhazel. She chanted:

"Eye of a newt and raven's wing,
Rise up, old Hoopler, and make them clean!"

The vacuum cleaner rose into the air and headed for the witches.
Va-room! It sucked up the dirt. But it also sucked up their socks.
And it sucked up the punch and the paper decorations.

"Make it stop!" yelled Hildy.
Cinderhazel ran across the ballroom, grabbed the trash can, and heaved it at
the Hoopler. Just then, the palace clock began to strike midnight.
With the twelfth dong, the witchy godmother's magic wore off.
POOF! Brooms and party goodies blew across the room.
The vacuum cleaner vanished, and – *ka-blunk* – Cinderhazel's broom
fell into cracked pieces on the floor.

The witches piled onto the mess,
screeching for their shoes, hats, brooms, and socks.
Just then, the biggest dirtball Cinderhazel had ever seen walked up to her.
"Euuuu! Yucky!" exclaimed Cinderhazel, grinning. "You're filthy!"
"That's my name, all right," said the dirtball. "Prince Filthy Alarming!
And, I must say, YOU are the dirtiest thing I've ever seen!"

"Thank you, your royal filthiness," Cinderhazel replied.
"Why have you been hiding so long?"
"Partly because I was told not to," said the Prince, "and partly because it's
such a bore dancing with a bunch of hoity-toity witches.
Yuck – they're so *clean!*"

"You know, I came here tonight because I was told not to," said Cinderhazel.
And she rubbed her nose with the hem of her skirt.
The Prince thought for a moment. "I would ask you to stick around," he said,
"but I'm not sure there's enough dirt for two of us."

"That's what you think!" cried Cinderhazel. "Check this out!"
She threw back her head. She crossed her eyes. She crossed her fingers.
She crossed her legs, and she whirled around like a tornado. Ka-*boom!*
An explosion of fireplace soot blew all the other witches out the door.

Not to be outdone, the Prince squinted and stuck out his tongue.
Ka-*blam!* Dirt showered down from the ceiling.
"Obviously," said Cinderhazel, "there's plenty of dirt around here.
But who says I want to stay?"

"Fine!" said the Prince. "Go away! I can see we can't stand each other!"
But Cinderhazel didn't go away.
And, of course, she and the Prince actually liked each other a lot.
In fact, they lived filthily ever after.

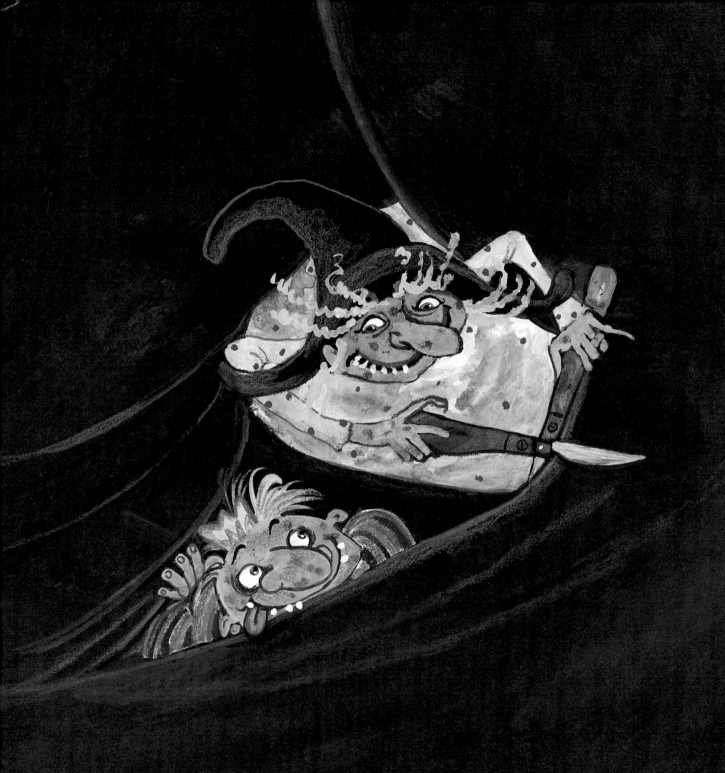

P.S. Cinderhazel never did have any glass slippers.
But on their first wedding anniversary, the Prince gave her
a more useful present: grass clippers.